# Barely Legal

### Barely Legal: A Serial

### VOL. 1

Kailin Gow

Barely Legal (Barely Legal Vol 1)
Published by RomanceOnTheGo.com, an
imprint of Sparklesoup Inc.
Copyright © 2014 Kailin Gow

For information, please contact:
Sparklesoup.com
First Edition.
Printed in the United States of America.

## DEDICATION

To My Readers, Betas, and Kailin Krusaders, Thank You for All Your Love, Support, and Encouragement. You are truly one of the most important reasons why I'm blessed beyond measure.

To women's shelters and their dedicated volunteers and staff. As a volunteer during my college and graduate years, I experienced firsthand the good these shelters provide women and their children. It is through them many lives have changed for the better.

# Prologue

## *Laura*

It wasn't the way I usually dressed to meet someone, especially someone new, but between my long hours at law school and the cryptic and unexpected text I received, I didn't really have much choice. I didn't have the luxury of going back to my apartment in Irvine, California to change so I wore a casual chic look of jeans, a sequined tank top and sneakers.

At least it was better than the sweats I usually wore when I spent the day in study hall and I had managed to pull the tangle of auburn curls that fell into my face back into a relatively neat ponytail.

Still, as I pulled up in front of the Crystal Towers in Los Angeles I wondered if my casual chic look wasn't a little bit too casual. Then again, I had no idea who I was meeting. The cryptic text message was simply signed,'P'.

I'd made a quick search of the tenants of the brand new building, but the tenant directory wasn't yet in place.

Biting my lip, I hesitated before stepping out of the car. I hated not knowing. I pulled my phone out and checked the message once more hoping to find a clue.

*Laura, how was your trip to Aspen? Relaxing, I bet. I know about you and Michael. This time, it went too far...but we know how it is in the throes of passion...sometimes you don't know when to stop. Now I know it really wasn't you who gave Michael his ultimate fantasy. You're not capable of it. Only a master could, which we know you are not. Be prepared Laura, Michael was well-known and graced many social magazines. The police will issue a public statement about his death in the next 48 hours. Soon the world will find out that beautiful, upright Michael Brooks died while having kinky sex in the hands of soon-to-be lawyer and unblemished Laura Turner. If you want to clear yourself, come to the top of the Crystal Towers in Los Angeles. – P*

Clear myself. I'd put way too much time and effort into my law school to have everything crash down on me now. If word got out that I was in any way involved with Michael's kinky death, the stain would remain attached to my reputation even once I was cleared of any wrong doing.

Getting out of the car, I looked up at the immense and shiny new building. Everything about it read rich and powerful, strong and intimidating. Well, I reassured myself as I straightened my shoulders, I will not let myself be intimidated.

# Chapter 1

Okay, so at first glance, I was thoroughly impressed with this new building. The architecture was strong and modern; straightforward lines with a definitive masculine air, but with an intense sense of drama and class. All glass and steel and chrome, the front foyer could have been cold and austere, but it somehow retained a bit of warmth. High above it all hung a striking crystal chandelier that was as strong in its beveled cuts as the large foyer demanded. Off to the right, behind the rich leather upholstered seating area, was a tall and narrow waterfall, and the sounds of the water crashing into the pool was the only sound in the huge space.

Other than that, the place was empty. Well, at least it wasn't some hole in the wall dump. With all the riches being flaunted, I had to assume I was going to be dealing with someone of substance... or at the very least someone influential.

Knowing there was little chance of getting more information, I still took a chance and headed to the directory on the wall by the bank of elevators, but it was completely empty. I looked around hoping to see a receptionist or clerk or guard; nothing. Nobody was on the main floor except for two young men washing the windows at the other end of the foyer.

Once more I pulled out my phone and considered calling my father, partly to let him know where I was, just in case things didn't turn out so great, and partly to see if he knew anything about this building and its tenants. It would be so easy for him to find out who this 'P' person was, but I'd already involved him in this whole sordid ordeal more than I wanted to. If ever this whole Michael story broke out, he could be implicated for giving me the address of the Brooks Aspen winter home.

Instead I punched Serena's name, but after half a dozen rings, I gave up. My best friend was probably with Sebastian anyway. Now that she was finally free of Price's clutches, she probably wanted to enjoy her newfound freedom with her new love. I couldn't really blame her. If I'd had someone like Sebastian waiting for me, I'd be locking myself away with him, too.

Her voicemail picked up and I stammered a second before leaving a message. "Serena, it's Laura. Look, I'm in Los Angeles, the Crystal Towers to be precise. Um... I don't really know what I'm getting into here. I got a strange message asking me to come here... something about Michael. Call me back the minute you have a chance. I think we're going to have a lot to talk about." I hesitated before cutting the connection. Should I have said more? But what?

I put my phone away and called for an elevator. The elevator doors opened immediately and I got in, but before I could punch in the button for the top floor, a couple stepped in and pressed it. Apparently we were all going to the same place.

Professionally attired in business suits, the woman appeared to be in her early thirties while the man seemed a few years older. Once again my casual chic look slapped me in the face. The woman's grey pinstriped suit was immaculate not to mention pricey, and her long dark hair was sleek in a prim and proper ponytail. Even her glasses were fashionable and professional.

9

The man also wore glasses, but they somehow seemed less fashionable. In fact, they almost looked retro, as did his sweater vest and bowtie over a crisp white buttoned down shirt. Though balding, he had pleasant features and an engaging smile.

After a quick glimpse at me, they turned to face the elevator doors.

"So what's this guy's background?" the woman said. "I mean, can he really replace Wilson? Do you really think he could play the role Wilson did?"

The bald man nodded. "Graduated top of the class; Harvard law. Spent two years as clerk at the Supreme Court then became a JAG and went back to work at Miley & Townshend. It was about time too. Thirty two years old and he finally decides to join the family law firm."

"What held him up?"

"Exploring the possibilities, I guess." The bald man looked pointedly at the woman. "You know, he used to be an MMA fighter."

"A lawyer who can throw a punch. That's a switch."

"And a lawyer who's in fucking good shape."

"I like the sound of that."

He shrugged. "It was back when he was a teen and in his early twenties. An injury kept him from competing."

"Hope it didn't keep him from keeping his body in tone."

"Can you get your head out of the gutter for just a minute?"

"Oh, please. I can see your fucking hard-on through those perfectly pleated slacks. Who do you think you're kidding? You're itching to fuck the guy more than I am."

He reddened as he pressed a catty grin. "Okay, so the guy is hot and I could fantasize about him all day, but that would hardly be productive, now, would it?"

She let out a throaty laugh and cocked a brow. "I would like to have the luxury of fantasizing about him, too, but from what I've heard, Peter Townshend only dates supermodels... maybe a few Hollywood starlets." She gave him an up and down sweep over her trendy glasses. "Don't want to burst your bubble, Brent, but I don't think you're his type."

"Oh, let me dream, will you?"

"Anyway, I hear he doesn't date anyone at work," she went on. "Thank God I'm married."

"What's that supposed to mean? You think he'd date you?"

"Don't sound so snide," she huffed. "If you were straight, you would know what a catch I am."

"Cheryl, darling, I may be gay, but I know when I'm out of my league, and, sweetheart, you're right out there with me. A man like Peter only goes for girls…" He tossed his head back at me. "…like her."

Smiling, I offered them an evasive shrug. I couldn't help wondering if they worked for this Peter Townshend. And as the elevator got closer and closer to the top floor, I couldn't help but wonder if that was where I was going too.

The elevator doors opened and the pair walked out. Cheryl offered me a last glimpse over her shoulder as she followed Brent to the offices to the right.

I headed straight to the large chrome reception desk and waited for the pretty blonde to look up at me. Wearing a clingy white halter-neck dress and large silver dangling earrings, she blended in with the chrome and glass décor. Even her long white fingernails were tipped with chrome.

"Yes, can I help you?" she finally turned to say.

For a second, I didn't really know what to say. I didn't even know who I was supposed to meet. I couldn't very well tell her I was there to meet with a mysterious Mr. P. For that matter, I didn't even know if it was a Mister. Finally, I simply opted to introduce myself, hoping she'd have the appropriate reaction.

"Hello, I'm Miss Turner."

"Oh, yes, Miss Turner. You can go right on in. He's expecting you."

He? It would have looked silly for me to ask who *he* is, but I desperately wanted to know before I pushed through that large chromed steel door. But of course, I just smiled and though I seriously felt underdressed all of a sudden, I walked, straight back and chin high, to that heavy door and pulled it open.

I was immediately hit with a blast of arctic chill. Surely someone had forgotten to properly adjust the air conditioning in there. I mean, I was only in there three seconds when my nipples perked up like high beams on a moonless night.

Of all the times for me to look so damned unprofessional. With only a thin cotton bra and the flimsy fabric of my tank top, I looked more like a stripper on break than a soon to be lawyer.

Regardless of all that, I walked in with a defiant tilt to my head. All of this mystery was starting to get to me and my mood was quickly shifting from curious and concerned, to angry and impatient. I'd often been told that my eyes turned dark blue like an angry sea when I was upset. Well, they must have been navy blue as I stormed into that office, walked up to the large plate of glass set over some half assed but undoubtedly expensive chrome sculpture and stared at the back of the large white leather seat that was turned to the wall of windows that looked down on L.A..

The arrogant bastard didn't even have the courtesy to turn around to greet me. No, he just sat there, high on his perch, looking down at the little people of L.A. like a Lord over his manor. Well, if he thought I was intimidated by his message, if he thought I was going to walk in there whimpering like some sap, he was in for a surprising earful. He wasn't the only one who could play games. If he was going to play the arrogant bastard with me, I was going to play scathing bitch to him.

"Well, Mr. P. I'm here, Laura Turner, and I can tell you, I am not too happy about having to put everything aside just to drive all the way to L.A. just so I can stare at the back of your chair. If you think threatening me is a good way of going about getting me to cooperate with whatever you've got in mind, you don't know me very well. I don't appreciate being threatened and I'm not going to stand for it."

With all that said, I stared at the back of the chair, waiting for a response, any response. None came.

"Did you hear me? Or are you going to hide behind there the whole time I'm here?"

Still nothing. The nerve!

Seething, I stomped my way around his desk, grabbed the chair and swung it around.

No one.

I heard my breath echo in the large office. Wallpapered in white leather, the room was sparsely furnished with only a few glass shelves on one wall, a large abstract painting in silver hues not yet hung and leaning against the wall below the shelves, and a glass topped bar on the other side.

There was nothing on the shelves, nothing on the glass topped desk and nothing on the bar.

"Hello?" I called out. "Is there anyone here? Mr. P., are you here?"

I was basically talking to myself and I suddenly felt like an idiot. Being up there in that empty office without knowing who knew so much about me left me feeling vulnerable and I didn't like it.

For the most part, I was usually in control. I knew where I was going and how I was going to get there. I liked to plan things out, know all the ins and outs of any situation, know all the options. I thought it was a big part of what would eventually make me a good lawyer. But the whole crypted message, a message that surely came from someone who knew me a little too well, knew about my past... it just gave me the creeps.

With a start, I turned. I heard a distinctive click and thought I'd heard the door close behind me, but there was still no one there.

Damn it. Bad enough I had to drive all the way down here, but to play this ghostly game...

"Miss Turner."

The deep and booming male voice filled the room, but seemed to come out of nowhere and everywhere at once.

Gritting my teeth, I turned back to the white leather seat expecting this phantom to just appear.

"What the hell is going on?"

"Forgive me, but I'll admit I'm a little surprised to see you here. I didn't think you would be able to make it on such short notice. Then again, I'm sure you understood the urgency of the situation. Time is of the essence, isn't it?"

"I don't appreciate these games, Mr. P. Where are you?"

His sardonic chuckle rumbled throughout the room and infuriated me all the more.

"Why don't you man up and show yourself? It's bad enough you had to send me a cryptic message..."

"Cryptic? Why, I thought I was perfectly clear and concise."

"Either way, the least you could do now is act like a normal human being and come out to meet me in person." I crossed my arms over my chest while my

17

eyes darted around the room hoping to catch him coming in.

"Feeling a little defiant today, aren't we, Miss Turner?" The question was smooth and seductive, as if my angry tone turned him on. "Your temper appears to be as fiery at that mane of auburn curls. I'd hate to come up against you in a court of law, Miss Turner. You must be a real tigress."

"You don't know the half of it."

"Well, allow me to congratulate you all the same. Seems like you're well on your way to becoming a lawyer. It mustn't have been easy."

"Not easy at all," I said. "But when all is said and done, I think I aced the bar exam. I should find out soon enough."

"A lawyer… you," he mused. "Fancy that."

Annoyed with his insinuation, I pursed my lips and swirled around trying to find where his voice was coming from. "Yeah," I said with a tight grin. "Fancy me living through three years of burying my head in one textbook after another, of one sleepless night after the other and with basically no sex life to speak of."

He laughed, a deep from the chest laugh. "What torture. When did you become such a

18

masochist? And why? Celibacy isn't for you, Miss
Turner. Why bother putting yourself through all that
pain and suffering?"

"Unlike you, who seem to get a kick out of
annoying the hell out of everyone, I like to help
people. As a lawyer I'll be in a position to help abused
women. I'll be able to help children find good
homes."

"Well, what do you know? An altruistic
lawyer. It's a dog eat dog world out there, Miss
Turner. A lawyer with too much heart and too many
fanciful ideals can get eaten alive out there."

"A smart lawyer with a conscious and a sense
of social obligation can get things done, Mr. P."

"I do love that fiery passion," he growled.
"And from what I can see, you're also cold... or might
you be excited?"

"Where are you, you pig?" I shouted as I
looked at all four walls for a clue to his hiding place. I
couldn't believe the nerve of the man, questioning my
integrity then turning around to make sexual
insinuations.

"Maybe you're both; a little cold and a little excited. I've been told my voice has that effect on women."

I felt the blood rush to my face as I glimpsed down at my nipples poking through the fabric that clung way too much to my breasts. Looking at me, no one would ever guess I was about to be a lawyer.

Then again, with that aggravating, yet sexy voice making such remarks, a part of me didn't feel like a lawyer at all. As much as I hated the mystery he was keeping, I was kind of thrilled by it too.

"Laura," his soft, deep voice called out.

Damn, if it wasn't the sexiest voice I'd ever heard. Just the sound of my name on that soft, velvety voice was enough to send a pleasurable tingle throughout my body.

"Laura Turner."

His voice shook the walls and vibrated against my body, feeling me, and touching me in such a wildly wicked way. At that moment, I didn't care who this man was. It didn't matter what he looked like. It didn't matter whether he was young or old, or whether he was fat or short. The man had a voice that could make any woman want to tear her clothes off. If he continued as he was, that was exactly what I was apt to do.

"Who are you?" I called out, desperate to get an answer before I made a fool of myself. What was he hiding? Was he hideous and afraid of anyone looking at him? Was he crippled? From the conversation two of his associates were having in the elevator, it seemed he was quite attractive. Then why didn't he show himself to me?

"A man who is only looking out for your best interest, my dear Laura."

"A man who goes by what name?"

"At this firm, they call me Mr. Townshend, but you can call me Peter."

"And how are we connected? Why did you contact me?"

"Ah, just like a lawyer to ask so many questions. Don't be too impatient, Laura. Everything in its own sweet time. For now, what you need to concentrate on are the two days that remain before your name and your nasty little deeds are splattered across the pages of every rag in this country. Michael Brooks was very well known. Imagine how shocked the public will be to hear how he died... and at whose hands."

"But I had nothing to do with..."

"Two days, Laura. The press doesn't care if you had anything to do with it or not. Implicating you simply because you were said to be in Michael's presence at the time of his death is enough to break your career before it even has a chance to get off the ground. So I want you to listen to me well."

My hands shook with rage and nervous energy at the thought of all that wasted time studying just to have it all go down the drain because of people's suspicions and the need for drama in the media..

"Listen to me carefully, Laura, because your whole future and the reputation of your family's name and business is riding on your understanding of my instructions. As of today, you will move into the Clarington building across the street. You'll find everything you need in room 411. If you'll look right in front of you, you'll find the key."

I looked around and couldn't see anything.

"On top of the bar."

I walked to the bar and finally spotted the silver key attached to a small acrylic clear key ring with a strange insignia on it. I reached out to the clear glass topped bar and grabbed it, though I still had reservations about his request.

"In the room reserved for you," he said, "you'll also find further instructions."

"Hold on a minute here. Why should I go stay there? I have my own apartment, not to mention my life back in Irvine."

"You won't have much of a life to go back to, if you don't follow my instructions."

"But, my..."

"Two days, Laura. Can you not sacrifice two days to save your precious future? Do you not have the passion it takes to save your career? If you don't then how can you ever hope to be able to help others?"

"Two days? You want me to live across the street for two days? I didn't even bring anything, no change of clothes, no toothbrush. I don't have..."

"I told you. Everything you need is in room 411."

I grunted my displeasure, but still shoved the key ring in my jean pocket. "Can you at least come out and show yourself? I'd like to know who I'm dealing with."

"All in due time, Laura. For now, you have all the information you need."

"Will we speak again?"

He let out a soft sigh and an amused chuckle. "Of course we will, Laura. When the time is right. I make people appear and disappear, and I assure you, I'll reappear in your life when the time is right. Don't be too surprised, however, if you're not too happy about the circumstances surrounding that next appearance."

# Chapter 2

With the key in my hand, I walked out of the chilly office and just stood by the closed door, too stunned to do anything. What had I just gotten myself into? Some strange man had just asked me to move into an apartment and I was expected to do what was told. Was I really going to follow his orders so meekly?

I thought of that message... I didn't really have a choice.

Who did that man think he was anyway? I fumed.

Peter Townshend, that's who. Peter Townshend. But who was Peter Townshend and how was he connected with me? The people on the elevator hadn't really given much away about the man, other than his fine physical appearance.

I usually had a memory like a steel trap, especially where people were concerned. Ever since I could remember, I'd had a knack for remembering people's names. The awkward and sometimes embarrassing moment of staring at someone as I tried to remember their name was something I'd never experienced... never or at least that I'm aware of. It would take something drastic like a head trauma to make me forget something or someone.

So if this Peter Townshend was a part of my past, how come the name didn't ring a bell? Not even a little tinkling?

On the other hand, as his voice echoed in my mind, I realized that there was something vaguely familiar about it. I'd heard that voice before, or one just like it, but I was far from remembering when or where.

Of course, if we had met some years before, it would explain his mysterious claim of knowing me. That, or someone had leaked some highly personal information about me.

Why, I couldn't fathom.

Finally breaking out of my stupor, I pulled out my phone and searched the internet for a Peter Townshend. Surely there would be something pertinent about such a rich and powerful man. I found several articles about an eighty year old Peter

Townshend who headed a prestigious law firm in Boston. Every article touted his talent in the courtroom, especially with regards to his last trial which had garnered him much publicity. The articles also listed his past successful cases, but said very little on his private life other than he'd married young and had had two children and a few grandchildren to which he'd left everything upon his death last May.

My next search attempt was for an MMA fighter named Peter or Pete Townshend, but that search resulted in no matches at all.

"Great," I muttered. A mysterious and faceless man with no internet trail whatsoever. Who, in this day and age, didn't have something about them somewhere on the internet?

A false name, I concluded. He must have used an alias, but it could be anything.

I stashed my phone away and headed back to the reception desk hoping to draw some information from the pert blonde. "Hi, I'm sorry to bother you, but, I'm just in awe of this building. It's so original and unique, so modern and… masculine. I don't think I've ever seen anything quite like it. Was it built recently?"

The pretty blonde looked up at me and shrugged. "Can't help you there. I just started working here a month ago. From what I can see, everything looks new, but I couldn't tell you when it was built."

"It seems strangely vacant for such an beautiful building. I guess the rent here must be astronomical. Maybe that's why they're having such a hard time renting out office space."

"I guess. I really wouldn't know about that. Numbers really aren't my thing. I just stick to answering the phones, greeting people and running the odd errand here and there for Mr. Townshend."

"Errands? Really? That's so… retro. So fifties."

The blonde looked at me with a blank stare and tilted her head to the side.

Oh, for heaven's sake, read a little Gloria Steinem or something, I wanted to say. "I thought the days of bringing coffee and getting the dry cleaning for the boss were over."

She shrugged. "I don't mind. I'm paid to do what he asks. Doesn't really matter much to me."

No, of course not. "It seems that this law firm is the only tenant in the whole building. That's a little peculiar."

"Well, I do know that we're the only one on this floor." She looked up at the ceiling. "I think we may even take up the floor above, but, other than that, I've never stepped off on any other floor, so I really wouldn't know if there's anyone there or not."

"The firm takes up the whole floor?"

"Yep."

I leaned over the desk and whispered, "But it's so quiet up here. There's no running around, no frenzied rush for depositions, or frantic pacing in anticipation of a verdict. Where are all the lawyers?"

The blonde looked at me with bored eyes. "They're here and there. Some have meetings outside our offices, others are already in the midst of a meeting in the board room. Things like that. There are at least thirty-five lawyers that I know about. When Mr. Townshend passed, the firm was broken up into different areas of practice. Peter, Mr. Townshend's grandson, took over the Los Angeles location. He..." She stopped suddenly and looked away as a pink blush quickly colored her cheeks.

I shook my head in disbelief. It seemed this girl had just as much of a crush on this mysterious Peter Townshend as the people in the elevator had. Apparently, men and women fell head over heels for this guy.

Was he really that great?

"Peter Townshend likes to do things a little unconventionally," the girl finally said.

"I'll say," I snapped. I was still angry about my *unconventional* meeting with him. What a strange and impersonal way of meeting someone. I wanted to ask the receptionist why he'd remained hidden from me. Why he hadn't met me face to face instead of hiding behind a wall?

Maybe the pretty blonde didn't even realize just how unconventional her boss really was.

"Is there something..." I hesitated as I searched for the right word. "My meeting with him was just so odd. I've never had such a peculiar experience in my life. Is there something... wrong with him? Something physical that makes him... shy?"

"No, Miss Turner. Absolutely nothing." Once again, the young girl blushed. "He's positively the most flawless man I've ever seen. So perfect in every way."

"So then why the…"

The phone rang, cutting me off and the blonde held up one perfectly manicure finger as she picked up.

"Yes. Yes, sir, she's still here. She's standing right in front of my desk." She looked up at me with authoritative eyes. "Yes, Mr. Townshend. I'll let her know. Yes. I'll do just that." She hung up and came around the desk.

Stunned, I stared at the impossibly tall girl. Her thin frame was made all the more fragile by the enormity of her gravity-defying boobs. It wasn't hard to imagine the perfect children this gorgeous young woman and the mysterious and apparently perfect Townshend would make.

The young woman grabbed my arm with surprising strength and yanked me toward the elevator.

"Hey, what's going on? What are you doing?" I called out.

"Just following strict orders," the girl said. "I am to show you out of the office and tell you that you need to be in room 411 in ten minutes. If not, I'm fired."

"Fired? He can't fire you for something like that."

"I told you; he's very unconventional. If he wants to fire me, he'll fire me. Besides, he's a lawyer. If he wants to get around a wrongful termination suit, believe me, he'll find his way around it, and if he can't, he'll keep me in litigation until I run out of money, which wouldn't be too long. Don't get me wrong. The salary here is great. Mr. Townshend is a very generous man. But..." She kicked up a heel. "I do love my Jimmy Choos."

Fuming at the arrogance of this guy, I tried to wring my arm free as I followed the girl. "Look, um..."

"Ana. My name is Ana."

"Look, Ana, I'm sorry I put your job on the line. I didn't realize it was so important I be there so quickly." Looking over my shoulder at the distant steel door to Peter Townshend's office, I added. "And I didn't realize we were dealing with an ego maniac."

"He's not that bad, and, don't worry about it, Laura. Following strict orders comes with the territory. I knew what I was getting into when I took this job. Mr. Townshend is generous, but he expects results for that generosity."

Ana said my name with such familiarity, as if we'd known each other for ages. Had I introduced herself as Laura Turner or simply Miss Turner?

"You know my name," I ventured.

"Of course I do."

What else do you know? I wanted to ask.

At the elevator Ana stopped and finally released her death grip on my arm. Staring at her, I willed her to say more, to tell me what she knew about the mysterious Peter Townshend. If I had a clue about what I was getting into, I wouldn't be so jittery and jumpy.

I would also be better prepared for our next encounter.

Maybe Ana knew what Peter knew about me. Maybe everyone here knew. I mustered up the courage to ask, and just as I took in a breath and parted my lips to put the question forth, Ana gave me an unceremonious shove into the elevator.

"You'll love the Clarington. It's a beautiful building with spectacular apartments. It's on the same street as we are, but two blocks south of here. The

Clarington. You can't miss it." She pressed the button for the ground floor. "Now go."

The elevator doors closed and I was alone; alone with my thoughts of my increasingly bizarre meeting with this Peter Townshend. Everything about the meeting was strange, from the empty office building right down to the forceful yet beautiful receptionist.

When the doors opened onto the lobby, my adrenaline was pumping with such fury that I almost ran out of the elevator, prepared to run the two blocks to this Clarington building. Stopping myself, I realized I'd left my car in the parking garage below. I pressed the appropriate button and the elevator brought me down and opened onto the pitch black parking area.

"This just keeps getting better," I muttered as I pulled a small flashlight out of my bag and flicked it on, bathing the dark garage in a clear blue light. My heart pounding, I directed the light to the right where I'd left my car and took long quick strides to get to it.

In the distance I heard a strange hollow sound and rushed to pull my car door open. It was locked. Of course it was locked. I always locked my car door, but with my growing panic, I repeatedly tugged on it anyway.

Taking in a deep breath that was far from calming, I directed my flashlight into my bag to find my keys. I had forever followed the advice once given to me to always have my keys in hand prior to entering an underground parking garage.

Of all the times to ignore that advice, I chose this one. I fumbled to get my keys out and shoved the car key into the keyhole, but just as I unlocked it and pulled the door open, the hollow ping sounded again, this time much closer.

I gladly welcomed the dim light that turned on inside the car and hopped in, eager to get out of the eerie setting and back onto the street, but in my haste I dropped the keys to the floor of the car.

"Damn it," I swore as I kicked my leg out to keep the door ajar so as not to turn out the inside light. "Calm down. Just calm down."

My words had no effect on my nerves as I doubled over to try to retrieve the keys from under my seat.

The sound of footsteps echoed nearby, too close. I sat up to close the door, but something blocked it from closing completely and I let out a little yelp of fear. Frantic, I tried again and this time the door slammed shut and I slammed my fist on the button to lock it, controlling the scream that rose to my throat and begged to be released.

I reached down again, grabbed the set of keys, and shoved the car key in the ignition, quickly turning it to get the headlights on. Nothing. No one.

The ping sound echoed again and I realized it was probably an air conditioning unit or something like that. It was far away and constant.

*I'm just spooking myself for no good reason.*

I put the transmission in reverse and backed out then headed for the exit. Once outside I let out a long cool breath.

The entire ordeal was starting to creep me out, but I didn't want to lose my cool. I had to stay calm.

Following Ana's instructions, I drove two blocks south and came to the Clarington building. Indeed it was spectacular. Tall pillars adorned with ornate scrolls guarded the entrance as did the uniformed doorman waiting to greet residents and guests. There was almost something Manhattan about it.

Unwilling to see another underground parking for the moment, I opted to leave my car on the street. After taking a moment to shake off the remnants of fear that still clung to me, I got out and headed for the door.

"May I be of assistance, Miss?" the tall and imposing doorman said. His avuncular smile seemed to hide something, like he knew something he shouldn't.

If things continued at this rate, I would soon be a paranoid neurotic incapable of any clear thought. Smiling, I held up the key that dangled from the acrylic keychain. "I'm looking for apartment 411."

"Indeed. The elevators are right through the lobby on your left," he said as he pushed the door open and waved me in.

"Thank you."

In the grand lobby, I took a moment to breathe it all in. The place felt more like a luxury hotel than an apartment building. Exquisite artwork lined the walls and the seating area was furnished with a modern take on Louis XVI chairs upholstered in a beautiful rose and gold striped damask.

I found the elevator, which was modern, but with an art deco touch, and I was charmed once more. Spending two days in such a luxurious building might not turn out to be so bad after all. In fact, I could easily get accustomed to living in such a grand place.

Already, I detected a spring in my step since entering the building, and my chin seemed to tilt up a little higher than usual. The fear and panic brought on by the dark garage were a thing of the past as I looked forward to the next two days.

Watch yourself, I silently warned. *You don't want to get all high and mighty because you have a temporary stylish address.*

When the elevator reached the fourth floor I got out and was once again impressed. The wide hallway was painted in muted tones of gold and bronze. A delicate wall mounted lighting fixture was set beside each door, with the same style of fixture echoed on the ceiling.

It was all so plush and luxurious, and I was increasingly eager to see the apartment itself. I turned to the right and strolled to room 411, taking in the occasional work of art that adorned the walls.

"So what is the big secret all about, Mr. Peter Townshend?" I said as I slipped the key in the keyhole above the elegant antique doorknob. I pushed the door open to find a short corridor that led into the apartment.

To my right the dining area welcomed me with a vase filled with vividly colored spring flowers and the living room beyond it was elegantly furnished with a curved leather sofa and two acrylic modern versions of Hepplewhite chairs set around a glass topped coffee table. Though pretty and tasteful, there was nothing really extraordinary about it.

I turned my attention to the bedroom. It was much larger than my room back in Irvine and decidedly more luxurious. My eye was immediately drawn the large window where the blazing afternoon sun streamed in through the apple green sheer curtains, bathing the room in brilliant light. Back in Irvine, my bedroom window looked out onto a shaded parking lot leaving my room in constant gloom.

While the fourth floor view wasn't spectacular, it was pleasant.

The big king sized bed took up the center of the room and was piled high with beautiful pillows in various shades of apple green. The creamy white comforter was soft and billowy. It was all so chic and expensive. The walnut commode, topped with a vase of fresh white roses, offered storage space and an elegant sense of style. In the first drawer I found soft and silky panties, in the second a rainbow of bras and in the third a variety of very small nighties.

"We're getting a little too intimate, aren't we, Mr. Townshend?"

Still, there was nothing particularly special about the room. For all the mystery that surrounded Peter Townshend, the room lacked the climatic resolution to it all. I don't know what I had expected, exactly, but I had expected more.

Opening the closet door, I walked in, hoping to find something more interesting, something more telling about the man and his intentions. Lined with cocktail dresses, a few gowns and an array of slacks and shirts, the wardrobe was a veritable who's who of the fashion world. Jacobs, Wang, McCartney, and on and on. And at the far end, shelves upon shelves of the most beautiful shoes I'd ever laid eyes on; black pumps, red stilettos, moss green sling backs and baby blue peeptoes. Every color and every style imaginable.

Kicking off my running shoes, I picked up a pair of Zanotti's fringed open toe booties and tried them on. I instantly went from casual chic to sexy chic. "I like your style, Mr. Townshend."

Keeping the beloved booties on, I turned to my right to find a series of small drawers; belts, scarves, bangles and more. Everything for the forward thinking fashionista.

"Looks like you really did think of everything, Mr. Townshend." I picked up a glittering crystal encrusted cuff and slipped it on. "Yes, and you thought of everything just right. I couldn't have chosen better if I'd gone out shopping myself."

My eyes darted around the large closet. It was almost too much.

"It's like getting set free in a candy store. I love it all."

I reached out for a perfect pair of periwinkle blue sandals and smelled the fine Italian leather then reached out to pet the soft and supple suede of a tan pump.

*I wonder if I get to keep these when all is said in done.*

Satisfied that my wardrobe was well taken care of, I headed to the bathroom. The large step-in tub was lined with bottles of fragrant beads, oils and salts and in the center of it all, a large bowl of fresh cut perfect white calla lilies.

Above the ceramique countertop was a large mirror trimmed with a gold braid and flanked by two compartments. In one compartment she found an array of cosmetics; half a dozen shades of lipstick, pink, peach, cherry red, persimmon, coral and magenta, several shades of eye shadow, an eyeliner and mascara. Housed in the other compartment were an assortment of salon shampoos and conditioners, and styling products. There were several brushes, combs and hair accessories. Everything else a girl needed to get ready to go out was in the top drawer.

Everything, he'd really thought of everything. I huffed and berated myself for being so naïve and easily impressed. He probably had Ana go out and shop for all this. Only another woman could think of so many little details.

Walking back into the living room, I checked my watch. I'd left the office ten minutes ago.

So why the big rush to have me in room 411 within ten minutes? More of his unconventional way of doing things? He'd mentioned I'd find further instructions, but there was nothing.

Just as I was about to chock it up to another mystery, there was a knock at the door.

"Punctual, this Mr. Townshend. Ten minutes sharp."

I opened the door to find no one there, only a small black bag at the door step. The hall was empty without even a sign of anyone passing by.

Mysterious even in the way he gives me instructions, I mused. Fine. At this point I realized there was probably little that could surprise me. I'd just have to give into the game and go with it. I picked up the large suede bag, surprised by the weight.

Inside my new posh apartment, I sat on the butter soft leather sofa and set the little black bag on the coffee table in front of me, trying to guess what it could possibly contain. A bottle of wine? A book?

The bag was tied with a silk cord which I tugged on to release the bow. With both hands on either side of the bag, I pulled it down and gasped as the contents were revealed.

Mirroring the exact color of my skin was a wax mold of a woman's breasts. Round and heavy with perked up nipples and even the tiny scar on the underside of the left breast.

It was the perfect mold of my breasts.

# Chapter 3

I stared at my breasts with a touch of amusement. There was something rather odd about gazing upon my own breasts sitting there on the coffee table.

"Not bad," I said with a touch of pride.

At the back of my mind, however, was one question; when had I had a mold of my breasts made… and why? Surely it was a process that was difficult to forget. Frowning I pulled the pair out of the bag and turned it over looking for a note or clue. When I found nothing, I rummaged through the bottom of the bag. Still nothing.

"Okay, Mr. Peter. I think you forgot something." Setting the breasts down, I headed to the kitchen and rummaged through the cupboards. Plenty of wholesome and nutritious food, just enough dishes, glasses, cups and flatware, and a minimal amount of pots and pans, but still no message regarding instructions.

I returned to the bedroom, my favorite room by far. Like steel to a magnet, I was drawn to the closet. Such a wardrobe, a wardrobe I never would have even dreamed of.

With my luck, half of it wouldn't even fit me.

"So let's give a few of them a try."

My first choice was a long sleeved black mini dress. I threw off my jeans and tank top and slipped the snug dress on.

"Like a glove," I murmured as I admired myself in the mirror. "And what shall we pair this magnificent mini dress with? A gladiator sandal? No. A classic but sexy black pump? No."

I slipped my fingers under the leather straps of pair of silver sandals embellished with crushed crystals. "Come to mama, my pretties."

With the sandals secured on my feet, I admired myself once more. "All that's missing is a knight in shining armor." I puckered my lips. "Hello, handsome," I whispered to my reflection. "Care for a drink?"

Swirling around to a beat to no song in particular, I danced and swayed my hips. Who would have thought a simple dress could do so much to brighten a mood?

"Okay," I finally said. "Get over yourself." I turned to the other dresses just waiting for me in the closet. "There are dozens more to try on."

Every dress fit me perfectly, even the gowns were of the right length with the appropriate heel. I was elegant and sophisticated in Reem Acra perfect pink strapless gown and stunning in a Dolce and Gabbana feminine tuxedo with a short open jacket over a black lace shirt with satin trim. The slacks were sophisticated and sexy, as if tailored specifically for me as though Mr. Townshend knew my body so very well. The thought sent an unexpected pleasurable shiver down my spine, as I imagined his hands over all me, feeling and memorizing every inch of me. A man who puts that much detail and attention into a woman's wardrobe, who was straight and as dominant as Mr. Townshend seems, is a man who appreciates women. It made the mysterious Peter even more tantalizing yet frustrating. Who was he, and how did he know my body so well?

There was something for every conceivable occasion. Even a cute pair of denim shorts with a playful puffy sleeved shirt and whimsical tennis shoes for a picnic in the park.

"You have great taste, Mr. Townshend. I couldn't have picked a better wardrobe myself... had I your budget of course."

I pulled out a striking navy dress with a plunging neckline and pulled it on just as the doorbell rang. Taking a second to check myself in the mirror, I adjusted the skirt and ran out just as the impatient visitor knocked on the door.

"Coming," I chimed. This time I checked though the peephole first. A pretty African American girl with long straight hair and velvety mocha skin stood there waiting. Her big brown eyes and full lips gave her a quiet and subtle sex appeal.

I opened the door only to find that the girl's body screamed loud and clear sex appeal. She was my height, but her neck was longer, graceful like a swan's, while the rest of her body was curvaceous, yet slim.

"Hi, I know we don't know each other, but I'm your new neighbor. I just move in a week ago, and, girl, I'm in a jam. I invited this really cool guy to come over for some soft music and appetizers... you know, a little wine and cheese type of deal, but, girl, I was so excited about this night with this hot new guy that I went all dumb ass and forgot to buy the wine. If you have just a simple bottle of red, or a nice bottle of white, I'd owe you one big time."

"Um, I'm not sure if I have any wine. I could go check."

"You have no idea how much I'd appreciate that. I mean, I don't want this guy to think I'm that air headed, you know?"

I opened the door wider and waved my neighbor in. "Come in, um...

"Camille," she said with a warm smile. "Camille Johnson."

"And I'm Laura. Come in. If there is any, you can choose the bottle you like."

"Thanks."

"What kind of cheese did you buy?" I asked as I led Camille to my new kitchen.

"Oh, nothing too fancy. An Asiago, a little Neufchatel and a good Brie."

I opened the refrigerator door. "Let's see what we have here."

For sure, I must have blushed all the way down to my toes. The top shelf had several whipped cream canisters, two bottles of chocolate syrup and the bottom shelf held a variety of drinks.

"Looks like you're ready for a fun party of your own, girlfriend," Camille said with a throaty laugh. "Maybe I should ditch my wine and cheese and get me some of that syrup and whipped cream instead."

I shut the refrigerator door. "I don't know where my head is at," I said, hitting the heel of my hand against the side of my head. I'd noticed a good sized refrigerated wine cellar tucked unassumingly beside the large armoire in the living room. "Follow me."

In front of the impressive wine cellar that easily housed two hundred bottles, I smiled. "Now that's more like it."

"I'll say," Camille let out as she pulled out a tempting Bordeaux.

"Red or white?" I said as I looked at the impressive assortment. Even my father, a wine connoisseur, would be impressed by the selection. From Chardonnays to Chiantis to Merlots and Pinot Noir, and everything in between.

"Red," Camille said. "I'll try to be reasonable and go with something I can afford... let's say, this 1992 Merlot."

"I don't really know all that much about wine, but I think this white Sauvignon would be great with the cheeses you mentioned," I said.

"How much do you think a bottle like that goes for?" Camille dug into the pocket of her skin tight jeans and pulled out a few bills. "Think twenty bucks will cover it?"

"Take it," I said. "Consider it a welcome to the neighborhood gift."

Camille's brow shot up. "For real?"

"Sure."

"I won't forget this."

Instantly liking my new neighbor, I walked her to the door. "Anytime. Maybe we'll have more time to chat the next time."

"Will do. I'll let you know how my night of wine and cheese goes." Camille stepped out, but poked her head back in before I could shut the door. "If you let me know how your night of syrup and cream turn out," she said with a playful wink.

I just laughed and closed the door behind her. Great. Camille was the first person I'd met in the building and this was the impression I'd made on her. She probably thought I was into some kinky, weird sex.

Heading back into the bedroom to take off the navy dress, I immediately noticed something different. Something was out of place. Something had changed since I'd left to open the door for Camille.

Hadn't I closed the closet door before heading out?

Feeling a little frustrated, I shook my head. Maybe I hadn't, but I was nonetheless surprised to see it wide open. Walking into the closet, my eyes turned directly to a blue woven silk tie draped over a wooden hanger.

Now I know that wasn't there before, I thought.

Maybe in my eagerness to see all the pretty dresses and try on the sexy shoes, I'd simply overlooked it. I'm going to be a lawyer, for heaven's sake.

*I'm not supposed to overlook something that is so blatantly obvious, especially when I'm here looking for clues.*

Pursing my lips, I pulled the tie off the hanger and fingered the fine fabric. The subtle tone on tone diamond pattern was barely distinguishable from afar, but distinct up close. Every other diamond had a daisy in it, also tone on tone. I'd seen the pattern before, but couldn't quite recall where or when.

"How could I have overlooked it?" I muttered, still unable to believe it. I walked back into the bedroom and looked around to see if anything else had changed. At first glance, everything seemed exactly the same as when I'd left it, but I no longer trusted my first glance. I took the time to re-examine the whole room and still found nothing out of place.

"So if that tie wasn't in there before, how did it get there?"

Stretching the tie straight out, I realized that it was much longer than the average tie and also a bit wider. Curious to see the designer of the tie, I flipped it over and was surprised to find the embroidered initials instead:

P.T.

Peter Townshend. The ever mysterious and unconventional Peter Townshend.

"More mystery, Mr. Townshend?" I called out into the room, almost expecting him to answer me. I held the tie up. "Is this tie supposed to mean something to me? Because, if you think this should ring a bell, it doesn't. I have no idea who you are and what I should make of all this."

# Chapter 4

I'd often been told I had the patience of a saint, but at that moment, after scouring the apartment in search of a clue or anything that could lead to a semblance of instruction, my patience was running thin... unnervingly thin. If mister big shot thought I was just going to sit around and wait for some vague instructions to appear, he was dead wrong. There was only so much control over me I'd allow him, and he'd overstepped that boundary. Despite what he might think, I had a life. Okay, so maybe between studying and exams it wasn't much of a life at that very moment, but it was my own and I had control over it.

But the situation he'd left me in, as fabulous as the apartment was and as glorious as all the clothes were, was not my life.

Not quite sure where I intended to go, I reached for my purse, and though it clashed dramatically with the fabulous dress I had on, I headed for the door. My hand on the door knob, my cell phone rang. I pulled it out of my purse and looked at the screen. While I didn't recognize the number, I had a feeling in my gut. Who else could it be but my mysterious new stranger.

"Hello?" I said, keeping my tone authoritative and strong.

"How are you enjoying your stay so far?"

My heart clenched, almost as much as the area between my legs. That voice, so smooth and sexy, so masculine and velvety. I already felt like putty in his hands, willing to do whatever he asked of me, and I didn't like it one bit.

I took a second to collect myself and hoped to pull out a strong and assertive voice despite the sexual tension growing inside me. My breath was a little labored when I said, "You've got good taste. I'll give you that."

"I'm glad you like it. I put a lot of time into making sure everything was to your liking."

"I'll admit, it wouldn't be a lifestyle difficult to get accustomed to."

"I thought you'd appreciate a little luxury after all that hard work studying. I also had a feeling you'd be the kind of girl who enjoyed the finer things in life."

"That would all depend on your definition of 'finer things in life.'"

"Well, how about this for a definition; maintaining your reputation. Of course, I'm sure you have lifestyle standards you'd like to maintain... a minimum of creature comforts, but when all is said and done, your reputation is really all you have, isn't it? How can you ever hope to become a lawyer with a murder rap over your head?"

My heart clenched again, but this time it was painful. He was playing with my life, toying with it as if it were some insignificant plaything. My reputation would be in shambles if word of this got out. Even if it was proven that I'd had nothing to do with Michael's death, the stain would remain for a long time.

Pacing the living room, I tried to get my breathing under control because I felt like I was going to explode at any moment. I was angry, hurt, afraid and even more angry. "I don't appreciate the mocking tone you're using, Mr. Townshend. This isn't exactly a laughing matter."

"Forgive me if I gave you the impression I was mocking you. That's not my intention, believe me. I simply want to bring to mind what brought you to room 411 to begin with. I wouldn't want you to be blinded by the luxurious apartment and pretty clothes to the point of forgetting why you're there to begin with. We have an agreement, remember?"

"An agreement?"

"Forgotten so soon? Tsk, tsk. As a lawyer you'll need to pay more attention to what you say. You agreed to stay in room 411 for two entire days... that is until this murder investigation was over."

"Clearly I was under duress when I agreed." Storming back to the bedroom I threw my purse onto the bed and let out a loud huff of frustration. I hated this lack of control.

"Duress? Nice try, Miss Turner, but I was hardly forceful with you. I simply explained the situation as it stands and gave you a means of clearing yourself."

"Well, I'm beginning to think you can't help me with that anyway... you and all these silly games. Sending me here, and all the pretty clothes and... you said I'd find instructions, but there's nothing here." I grabbed the tie off the bed. "I found a custom made tie with the initials P.T. embroidered inside. I take it it's yours."

"Did the clothes fit you?"

"Perfectly, but that's beside the point."

"And I take it they're to your liking."

My jaw tightened. I didn't want to let him know how impressed I was with the wardrobe he'd selected for me, but it was flawless. He had impeccable taste, but I was certain he knew that already. "Like I said, you have good taste. I probably would have chosen all the clothes in that closet had I the money."

"It's no accident the dresses fit you so perfectly. Most of the pieces were made specifically for you while others were tailored to precise specification."

I cocked an impressed brow. "I haven't the faintest idea why you would go to so much trouble... maybe you have a little too much time on your hands, but the matter that concerns me now is this tie. Is it yours?"

"Aren't you a little curious to know how I came to know your measurements so well? The size of your breasts, the curve of your waist, the swell of your hips, the wealth of your perfectly round and firm ass."

I wasn't sure if I really wanted to know the answer to that one. Of course the question was burning at the back of my mind, but I knew his answer would be more playful than informative. "Tell me about the tie, Mr. Townshend. It's a rather peculiar tie. It's so much longer than a regular necktie. It's also broader. And I believe it's yours. Why do you refuse to answer me?"

"Don't trust those embroidered initials, Miss Turner. Looks can be deceiving sometimes."

"So, it's not your tie?"

"It's the designer's logo. Disappointed?"

"Just a little surprised, I guess. I mean, what are the chances that you send me to an apartment, furnish me with a glamorous wardrobe and just happen to find a strange looking tie that just so happens to have your initials embroidered on it, but it doesn't actually belong to you? What are the chances?"

"Life is full of amusing coincidences sometimes, isn't it?"

"Then if the tie isn't yours, what is it doing here amidst these beautiful clothes meant for me. Surely you don't expect me to wear it."

"Wear it? No, not exactly." The register of his voice fell to a deep and lusty level that practically drooled with sexuality.

"What exactly, then?" I bit my lip as I anticipated the answer.

"Although, when tied properly, it fits like a regular tie, this one is actually meant to serve a higher purpose. This tie becomes an instrument of pleasure; your pleasure, Miss Turner."

I gasped, though I shouldn't have been surprised. This was just the sort of thing such a mysterious man would do, though I couldn't imagine why he would leave it in my closet. Was he aware just how deserted my sex life was?

"Speechless?"

"Hardly," I said, quickly getting over the significance of the strange tie.

"Tell me," he said with a low and luscious voice that was driving me crazy. "Is the tie strong?"

"As much as a tie can be strong." The sensation of the tie in my hand suddenly took on a whole new meaning. If I wrapped my fingers around it, it was strong, almost hard.

"Is it flexible?"

"Of course."

"Is it firm?"

"Firm?" I fingered the fabric again and it suddenly wasn't a tie at all. My mind had completely side tracked and was envisioning horribly delicious and delectable things; things I shouldn't be thinking of at the moment. Things I shouldn't be thinking while on the phone with this strange man.

"Yes," he whispered. "Firm, yet soft."

"I guess."

"Pull on it. Does it stretch? Does it give a bit, all while still being able to hold a knot?"

"It looks like it might."

"Why not try it?"

"What do you mean?"

"For a smart, soon to be lawyer, you're acting a little innocent and naïve, aren't you?"

"Hardly," I said, suddenly feeling a little defensive.

"You're wearing a dress, right?"

"Yes."

"Run the tie around your calves."

Intrigue not only by his orders, but the tone in which he gave them, I obeyed. The silk was soft and smooth against my skin.

"Run it up to your thighs and pull it between your legs."

I sat on the very edge of the bed and pulled the silk tie between my thighs. The soft fabric rode between my legs with tantalizing friction.

"Is it soft?"

"Yes."

"Arousing?"

I didn't answer.

"Tug it up higher on your thigh."

I hesitated for just a moment as I realized where he was going with his commands. A part of me didn't want to give him the satisfaction of arousing me, but the other part of me was very curious about my own satisfaction. Would a simple tie do the trick?

Tugging the tie up higher on my thigh, the soft, silky fabric rubbed lightly against my panties and brought an interesting thrill to my clitoris.

"Good?"

Unable to verbally answer him, I simply nodded.

"I'll take that silence for a yes. Now, put your phone on speaker, and set it down."

The soft control of his voice added to my arousal as I followed his directions.

"Go a little faster. Pull the tie up between your legs just a little bit harder."

The added pressure caused me to gasp. I was horny, a lot hornier than I had thought. I guess these months of studying had left me in need, and I'd been ignoring that need.

"Do you feel how good that is?"

I couldn't answer him, but it did. It felt so good. I groaned, deep in my throat as the pleasure rose, and all that mattered was the sound of his voice and the sensation of the tie against my panties, now wet with my arousal.

"I like the sound of that," he said. He sounded just as aroused as I was. "I'm glad to hear that you're not only following my orders, but enjoying it as well. That groan was full of... promise."

Knowing that he was pleased, that he was aroused, fueled me. I wanted to please him. I wanted to turn him on. I wanted to promise him more.

"Are you close? Are you almost there?"

"Yes," I said in a breathy voice. I was surprisingly close

"You sound like you're just on the edge. Don't you just love that moment, that moment of heightened pleasure, just before it all explodes... when you hover, weightlessly, for that precious moment and all that matters is the climax to come?"

"Yes." The word was barely audible on my breath.

"I only wish I could see the rapture of this moment on your beautiful face. I want to see your face contort in pleasure, twist in ecstasy, relax with satisfaction."

I could only breathe as I closed my eyes and tugged harder on the tie.

"Ah," I shouted. I was so close, I was right there, hovering, just like he'd said, delighting in that moment of levity just before...

"Not yet, Laura. Not yet."

"Oh, my God. You can't be serious. Please," I pleaded, but I forced my hands to slow down.

"I want to hear you a moment longer. I want us to enjoy this exquisite pleasure just a moment longer."

"Oh, please. Let me..."

"Not yet."

"Oh, shit."

"No."

"Ah, God."

"Laura?"

"Peter!"

"Be a good girl," he whispered. His voice was a kiss all over my body, a kiss in the dark, on the most delicious part of my body, hot and hungry.

"Yes." It was just there, so tantalizing and so explosive. And the more he made me wait, the more explosive it would be. Something about Peter broke all of my reserve and control. Something...

"You're a good girl."

"Yes!"

"Now, my sweet Laura!"

"Ah, yes."

"Come now."

"Oh, my God!" I screamed as I fell back onto the bed and tugged the tie up into my crotch where my clitoris throbbed against it.

"Let me hear you."

"Ah, Peter." Catching my breath was almost impossible. My orgasm was so strong, so shattering. I clutched the tie with white knuckles, unwilling to let go of the precious garment. Staring blindly at the ceiling, I rejoiced in the slow ebb of my orgasm, thrilling with every last throb until it completely subsided leaving me only with one hell of a fantastic memory of this moment. What had just happened?

"That was an impressive climax," he groaned. His husky voice filled my room and I suddenly wished he was there, in the room, with his hands all over me, his lips, his body. "Your passionate cries still ring in my car."

"Your car?" I whispered through jagged breaths.

"Yes," he said with a faint chuckle. "I'm very pleased with how you followed my orders so explicitly. You didn't miss a step. In fact, you've even surpassed my expectation."

I smiled, though I didn't fully understand why. I liked the notion of pleasing him, but resented the control he had over me.

"I want to come by to see you now. I'll explain a few things to you. Would that be all right with you?"

All right? Oh my God, I think I'd die if he didn't come over.

"You're coming here straight from your office?" I had no idea why I even asked that question. Was I that eager to see him? Or was I afraid he'd be at the apartment before I could make myself presentable? I couldn't very well open the door for him in this state.

Could I?

All of a sudden it seemed so important I impress him, so much so, I actually felt self-conscious. I wanted to find a sexier dress, redo my hair, put on some perfume. This man with the incredible voice and confident take charge attitude was getting to me, challenging me in ways I haven't been challenged before.

"No," he said, shattering my anticipated race to get ready. "I'm just finishing up with a meeting on the other side of town. I left right after you headed for the Clarington and managed to rush the meeting just a bit. That's how eager I was to call you, to talk to you... to turn you on. I'm going to turn onto the freeway the moment I hang up, so should I be there in about half an hour."

"Oh." I couldn't hide my disappointment. I guess I was eager to have him there as soon as possible after all, no matter how unpresentable I was.

"Don't sound so glum. I'll be there soon enough, my sex vixen. You'll have just enough time to recover and get warmed up again."

My mind raced as I tried to find an explanation to my reaction to him, but none came. I just hated that he'd heard the disappointment in my voice. Shaking my head I stared at the phone on the bed beside me and wondered when I'd lost so much control over myself. When had I become such a mass of sexual energy that didn't care about consequences... and I was sure the consequences would come. He wouldn't let me forget the orgasm he'd just taken part in.

"In the meantime," he went on, seemingly cool and unruffled by the heat of the moment, "Why don't you change panties? I think you're in need of a fresh pair. I personally like the barely there silk ones. Feels like a petal against your skin, yet easy for me to tear off. Why make it complicated?"

A growl resonated from my belly all the way to the phone and was met with a chuckle.

"Don't get mad at me because you enjoyed it, Laura. It's perfectly all right that you be so aroused by all this. Don't be too hard on yourself."

I turned onto my side and looked at the phone. Just as much as I had enjoyed our little interlude, I was upset by it. I wanted to see him and touch him, but I also dreaded his arrival. The power he seemed to already have over me was a little too much and I wasn't sure I wanted to go where he was leading me.

But my body seemed primed and ready for more… hungry even.

"I realize I didn't properly stock your kitchen… nothing for an elegant and gourmet meal. How about I take you out for dinner?"

"Sounds good."

"Hungry?"

"Starved." I couldn't even remember what my last morsel of food was.

"Good. I've got quite an appetite myself. I'll see you soon."

"Just one last thing…" I knew I was being annoying, but I had to know.

"Yes?"

"The tie. Is it yours?"

"What do you think?"

"I think it is. I think your story about it being the designer's logo is bogus."

His deep and amused chuckle rumbled through the phone, so hearty and filled with lust, I felt a thrill ride up my thighs. "After the performance you just gave," he whispered, "I wish it was, Miss Turner. I truly wish it was."

# Chapter 5

After a quick shower, I pulled my hair back into a quick and easy bun, slipped into the body hugging red dress and found the perfect red lipstick to complete the elegant yet sexy look. All that and I still had ten minutes to kill before Peter Townshend arrived.

Peter Townshend... just the thought of his name sent a shiver through me. Was it the mystery that surrounded the man that had me captivated, or the orgasm he just gave me?

I was excited and anxious, and I went back to the mirror a dozen times to make sure everything was okay. Two soft curls had escaped the bun and brushed delicately against my skin. The dress was tight enough to show off my body, but not so low cut as to scream my growing need for a sexual encounter with this mysterious man.

Just as the doorbell rang, I slipped into a pair of four inch stilettos and hurried to the door.

Curiosity was high as I reached for the doorknob. What would he look like? Was he tall? Was he strongly built? Was he as handsome as his secretary had said? What if he wasn't?

At this point it hardly mattered. I wanted him. That sexy voice had been driving me crazy from the start and I longed to have him kiss me, touch me... make love to me. It'd been so long... far too long since I'd been with a man, and longer still since I'd been with such an exciting man. My body was thirsty for something good, and strong and compelling, and he was all that.

Yes. I turned the doorknob. I want whatever he has to offer. "You're early," I said with a teasing smile as I pulled open the door, ready to seduce the enigmatic Peter Townshend.

"Oh, my God. You're expecting someone," Camille said. Visibly upset, she glanced back at her apartment door and back at me.

"Camille. What's going on?"

"Look at you. You're obviously waiting for a date." She turned to walk away. "I... I won't bother you with my problems. I got myself into this mess and I'll get myself out."

I took a step into the hall, grabbed her wrist and pulled her into my apartment. "My date isn't due for another ten minutes. What's going on? What happened?"

Camille looked at me with fear in her big brown eyes. I saw in her the same fear and vulnerability I'd seen in Serena all those years ago. Obviously something had gone wrong with the night she'd planned. I guided her to the sofa and headed to the kitchen to pour her a glass of water. I also grabbed the box of paper tissue set atop the refrigerator.

As I sat in the lounge chair facing her, I set the glass down on the coffee table.

"Thanks," she whispered and took a delicate sip.

"Why don't you tell me what happened? Your date upset you, didn't he?"

Camille threw her face into her hands and cried, her shoulders shaking from the force of her sobs.

"Franklin."

"That's your date?" I pulled a tissue from the box and handed it to her.

She nodded and dabbed the tissue to the corner of her eyes. "He's such a smart guy... well educated, well mannered, well dressed. He comes from a really good family. His father is the CEO of some big, multi-million dollar company and his mother is a major share holder of a cosmetic company." Shaking her head, she stared straight ahead. "Right from the start, he said all the right things… all the things I wanted to hear. He was so sweet and so considerate. It was like he knew what I wanted before I could tell him. Oh, and Laura, he's just so damned handsome, so impossibly good looking. He's really the kind of man I barely dared allow myself to dream of meeting one day, and there he was, in my apartment, wanting me."

"Things didn't go so well?"

"The well-educated man from the very well to do family turned out to be a monster with hard and rough hands. I mean, an octopus with hands all over the place, grabbing and pinching and groping and… Don't get me wrong. I'm no virgin or nothing, but there's got to be a certain pace to these things, right?"

"Right."

"And he just dove in, didn't even give me a chance to take a breath. We didn't even have dinner. Just a few quick glass of wine." She looked down at the faded cotton dress. I just threw this old dress on to be decent as I came here. The dress I'd worn for my date with him is practically torn in two."

I reached for her hand and patted it gently. Men... they could be so insensitive at times. "I'm sorry your evening went so awry. That really sucks."

"You bet it sucks. I don't get it. I mean, if you'd have seen him, you would never think... He's tall and strong, but so soft spoken and gentle... so polite and gallant. I mean, he didn't have to go all monster on me. I was willing to get down with him, just not..." She burst into tears and reached for another tissue.

"Did he..." I didn't even want to say the word.

Sobbing, she nodded. "After only two glasses of wine, we started kissing... you know, making out. And, shit, but it was so good. His lips were so soft, but then it was like nothing was going fast enough for him. He yanked up my dress, tore off my panties and pinned me to the sofa then shove his fingers inside me. I told him to cool it down, to take it easy, but it just made him angrier, hungrier. He said I was just leading him on, but I wasn't. Why was he in such a rush?"

Not knowing what to say, I simply shook my head. I was heartbroken for her.

"When he pulled his fingers out and saw that I was wet, he called me a slut and a tease and a whore. He grabbed me by my hair, pulled me off the sofa and practically dragged me to my bedroom."

"Oh, Camille…"

"He pushed into me so hard… Damn it hurts. It hurts to the bone."

"Where is he now?"

She looked at me with renewed fear.

"He's sleeping it off. The minute he came and spilled his seed all over me, he fell over me like a dead weight and started snoring. I barely managed to crawl out from under him."

"Camille, he's still in your apartment?"

She nodded and looked down at her hands. "The idiot is cold drunk, and I don't know what to do. I don't want to go back in there. I don't ever want to see him again."

I patted her hand again and knew I had to do something. "Look, you stay here." I reached for my phone and put it in my pocket. I wanted to take a few photos that could possibly serve as evidence should the situation go that far. "Take a minute to collect your thoughts, to catch your breath and when I get back, we'll call the police. I don't want you to put that off for too long. It's important they get here fast enough."

"Why bother, Laura? It'll just be his word against mine. I mean, I willingly let him into my apartment. I willingly..."

"You didn't willingly get raped." I stood to leave.

"Laura," she called out.

I turned and saw the pain and shame in her eyes.

"This type of thing never happens to me. I'm a good judge of people. I'm going to be a lawyer, for heaven's sake. I know how to read people. I don't understand how I could have so misread him. I don't understand how I could have been so stupid and gullible."

"Don't talk like that, Camille. Men are too good at being deceptive for you to kick yourself over this. It's not your fault the guy's an asshole and good at hiding it."

"Well, watch me next time," she said through a sniffle. "I'll have a background check on the guy before I let him set foot in my place."

"I'm going to go make sure he doesn't snake his way out of there before the police get here."

"I don't know how to thank you for all this. You're too much."

"Don't worry about it. Take all the time you need to get yourself together."

Nodding, she looked at me. Hope and even a touch of admiration shone in her eyes, and she suddenly seemed so small and fragile, I wanted to just hold her in my arms and comfort her.

"I'll be back in a minute." I could hardly remember the last time I was so upset, so raging mad. My fist clenched the doorknob and I yanked the door open and stomped to Camille's door. The nerve of that man taking advantage of a young girl. I had half a mind to kick the damn guy's balls off. He deserved no better.

As I reached out for the doorknob of her apartment, I suddenly felt nervous and unsure. A drunk man with a bad temper was inside and I questioned the wisdom of entering alone. Camille said he was out cold... cold drunk.

Determined to make sure he stayed put, I took a deep invigorating breath, opened the door and stepped inside. Camille's apartment was dark and gloomy, and I tried to hold the door open with my foot as I reached out for the lamp in the corner. Just out of reach, I let go of the door and hurried to the lamp before it shut behind me.

I wasn't fast enough. The door quietly closed behind me, and when I switched on the light, it didn't work.

"Great," I muttered in the dark apartment.

But it's only when I heard a firm click, the distinctive click of a deadbolt being turned, that bile rose from the back of my throat and the hairs at the back of my neck prickled. My heart raced as I tried to find a way of negotiating with the large man with a rapist's mind. Would I be his next victim?

Coming into Camille's apartment alone could very well turn out to be my most regrettable move, but I was there and there was no turning back. I planted my feet firmly to the floor, ready to face him, despite the dark that cloaked Camille's apartment.

# Chapter 6

I took a step back while my hands searched for something... anything that could serve as a weapon, but there was nothing. I wasn't about to be his second victim of the night. If he wanted to attack me, to try to rape me, I'd make it as hard as I could for him.

Drunk, he should fall with one well-placed punch in the face. All I had to do was manage to get that punch in.

His footsteps approached, small little steps that were surprisingly light for the large man Camille had described. I took another step back and realized there were two sets of steps. One had a light clip sound while the other a scraping sound.

Had Camille mentioned someone else and I hadn't caught it? Another man?

Before I could find out, someone kicked the back of my knees from behind, and I fell forward. Hands pulled my hair back and roughly pushed my arms back. I heard a click and felt cold hard steel around my wrists. Was I just handcuffed? I flailed behind me, trying to elbow whoever was there. My elbow made contact with something soft. He grunted and groaned, a strangely delicate sound for a man

"Bitch. You'll be sorry you elbowed me in the ribs, but I'm the one who have you now."

I stopped dead in my tracks and listened more carefully to the voice... the whispered, husky voice of a woman.

"I told you it wouldn't be a problem."

Another familiar female voice, this one with a distinct British accent. "What do you want to do with her?" the Brit said.

The dark and sinister snicker that came from the first voice shook me. Whatever they had in mind, it wasn't going to be pleasant. I pulled my wrists around, twisting my waist to reach the console and ran my hand along the smooth surface, hoping once again to find a blunt object that could serve as a weapon; a candle holder, a vase, a statuette... anything. But the only thing I found was a pad of paper... completely useless paper.

"I want to know the truth," the first voice said. "Even if I have to beat it out of her."

"Hey, you're going to have to leave me out of that part. I'm not getting involved in anything violent."

"What do you want?" My shaky voice echoed in the silence that followed and I hated the sound of fear that shook every word.

A glaring light suddenly flicked on, blinding me while allowing my captures to view just how terrified I was.

"What do you want?" the first voice mimicked with a cruel snicker.

"Look," the Brit said. "I want nothing more to do with this. You never told me you'd take things this far."

"Think twice before you back out. You're already in deep with P.T. Leaving this job unfinished could cost you quite a bit. You wouldn't want to harm that career of yours, would you?"

P.T.? Oh, my God. Was Peter Townshend involved with this twisted game? Was he behind this whole crazy and deranged plot? I'd strangle him if he was.

"Look, I don't know what you guys want with me, but I'm not looking for trouble. Just let me…"

"Hear that? She's not looking for trouble. Dear, you found trouble the day you were born, and when you took away what was dearest to me, you found trouble big time, because I'm not about to let you wipe your hands off what you did."

The voice sounded familiar, so familiar. Every word brought me back to a time, to a place, but it was vague and blurred. The only thing I knew for certain, the time and place it brought me back to wasn't all that pleasant.

"You should have known better than to fuck with me, Laura."

She knew me. This wasn't just a random attack.

"Look, whatever I did, I'm sorry. I can't imagine what I could have done to make you abduct me."

A loud clap of laughter startled me. "Did you hear that? Abduct. Spoken like a true lawyer. We didn't abduct you, sweetie. You walked in here of your own volition."

Yes, I walked in on my own, but I came based on Camille's story. A story. Was that all it was? A story to get me in here? To trap me?

And where was Camille now? Maybe she didn't even live in this apartment or in this building.

The bright light came forward and I backed further into the apartment and came up to the back of a sofa.

"What did you do to Michael?"

"Michael?" I was stunned by the question. What did all this have to do with Michael?

The light came closer still, so fast, I didn't have time to react before a hand came out and slapped my face.

"Michael Brooks, you bitch! Did you forget him already? Did you forget what you did to him?"

"Hey, cool it," the Brit said. "There's no need to push her around. I'm sure if you just ask her, she'll tell you what you need to know."

"Shut up, bitch, and go hold her down. If she wants to play stupid and innocent, I'll show her what it's like to mess with someone like me because there isn't a chance in hell that she's getting out of here before I get an answer."

My heart pounded. That voice. That wild and demented voice. Only once before had I heard it in such a tone, so angry.

"Wait, I think you've got this all wrong."

"I don't get anything wrong, Laura. You were with him, you slut." She slapped me again, hard enough to knock me back a few steps.

"That's enough!" the Brit called out.

The lights flicked on and I stared at the women in front of me.

"Camille?"

"Sorry, babe. You look like a really nice girl. I didn't mean for things to go this far." Her eyes were filled with sorrow, but it did nothing to diminish the anger and sense of betrayal that took over me. Gone was the friendly California girl I thought I had befriended and in its place was a sophisticated street smart worldly woman with a British accent.

Though I'd only just met her, I'd felt an instant bond with her, an instant sisterhood. I couldn't believe it had all been a hoax, right from the beginning. The wine, the handsome guy, the rape... all a lie just to get me in her apartment. "Who are you?"

My eyes quickly fell on the other woman, the aggressive woman who'd slapped me, the angry woman who wanted answers.

"Big mistake, turning on that light.  Now she knows who I am."

Her sinister grin turned her beautiful face into a contorted mask of hatred and vengeance.

"Willow," I whispered in disbelief. Willow Brooks, Michael Brooks' sister.

# Chapter 7

"Willow," I said, genuinely surprised. "I haven't seen you and Michael for years. It's been what...five or six years?"

"Oh, stop with the innocent act, Laura. We all know what a wanton slut you are. And we all know you were the last one to see Michael alive."

"Wait, you've got this all wrong. I was nowhere..."

"Stop it!" Her shrill cry startled even Camille, if that was in fact her real name. "I know you were there! Stop with the higher than thou attitude, because you're not going to get away with this."

She was clearly hysterical, maniacal even. There was no reasoning with her. Her fingers clenched and unclenched repeatedly around the small flashlight she still held in her hand, still flashed in my face despite the overhead light.

Arguing with her would do no good, so I thought I'd try to bluff my way out. "What do you want to know?"

Her eyes narrowed. I'd never particularly liked Willow. She'd always been haughty, always above everyone... far above. But to look at her now, it was hard to believe she was the beautiful young socialite so many women envied and admired.

In truth, she was just a rich brat who thought the world revolved around her. Things had to go her way, or the people around her had to suffer her wrath.

"So you were with him."

"What if I was?"

"I should have known he'd go crawling back to you. Michael always had a thing for alley cats. He liked the power it gave him to be with someone so beneath him. Trash... something he could screw around with and toss aside without a moment's thought. That's all you've ever been to him... that is until you tricked him into falling for you."

I swallowed the ball of anger and repulsion that quickly built up in my throat. I'd known Michael a long time ago... a very long time, but it'd been a short lived and very secret liaison.

"Yes, sweet Laura. I know about your sordid little affair with my brother. You were the little tramp he just couldn't get enough of." She shrugged and glanced back at Camille. "If anything, my brother had questionable taste in women. If you'd only seen the young debutants and glamorous socialites who've thrown themselves at him over the years."

She brought her hate-filled gaze back at me. "Lord only knows why he chose you. And I'll admit I'm surprised to find out he was still into you... until his dying day, as it turned out. Look at you. You're a wannabe trying to act like you belong in a building like this, like you belong in a dress like that. You're all wrong for this kind of life, Laura. You're far beneath Michael's status. You and your slutty friend Serena think you can fuck your way into the billionaire's circles. Your father might be high and mighty in the food business, but it's not enough to grant you entry into the life of the obscenely rich... not even close."

From our very first encounter, when teens, Willow had shown immense resentment for me. I never really understood why. She was a beautiful and intelligent girl, so I knew it wasn't a matter of jealousy. At times I'd wondered if she wasn't overly possessive of her brother.

"You've got it all wrong."

"Nice try, but Michael told me."

Told you what, I wanted to ask.

"He was the best thing that could've ever happened to you and you blew him off. I never understood why he fell for you, but he did, and you just trampled all over him like a gutless rat."

I tried to think back on those years so long ago. I'd always considered we'd parted ways of mutual agreement. His life was going one way while mine was leading me elsewhere. If he'd been angry about the split, he never showed it.

"You know Michael had a purpose in life… and he also had a purpose in mine. He'd agreed, willingly agreed to go after Serena, to seduce her and to lure her away from Sebastian."

"Ah yes," I said with an irrepressible snicker. "Your beloved Sebastian. I'd forgotten just how obsessed you are with Bash."

"Bash is not an obsession. He's my destiny."

"He seems to think otherwise."

"I don't think you're in a position to talk smart, Laura. Bash is my destiny. He's just been sidetracked by that bitch. She brainwashed him. If you hadn't gotten in the way, Michael would have seduced Serena and Bash would have had no choice but to leave her and come running to me. You had no business snaking your way back into Michael's life. You knew he'd take you back, that he still loved you, but you know damn well that you don't want a life with him... that you don't love him. You ruined everything for nothing."

Willow knew nothing of what I felt for Michael. I thought I loved him once. That he was going to be the one. However, our relationship had been tumultuous and he'd led me into a world that was new and strange to me, while I led him into another that made me questioned who I was, but I'd always had great affection for him, and still had.

"You're living in a dream world, Willow. Whether Serena is in the picture or not, Sebastian wants nothing to do with you. Don't you get that?"

"Admit it, bitch. You deliberately set out to ruin everything for me. You went after Michael just to ruin my plans. You broke his heart when you left him back then and you just stepped into the picture to break it again, and to keep me from splitting up Serena and Bash."

"You've a fanciful imagination, Willow."

"Don't underestimate me, Laura. It could cost you dearly. You've already pushed me to turn to another option to get Bash away from Serena, an option I was reluctant to put into play. I could get P.T. on my side. I know that he wants this separation just as much as I do."

P.T.? Did Willow know who Peter Townshend was? And so intimately that she would turn to him for such a plot?

"You seem surprised to learn that I know him. Know this, Laura; in the world of bondage, we tend to know each other a lot. And, yes, P.T. has always been my alternative plan if Michael failed to woo Serena away from Bash. I would have preferred to avoid any collusion with P.T., but sometimes things just don't go my way."

I stared at her, dumbfounded, as I tried to make the connection between her and the man who'd just brought me to orgasm over the phone.

She took a menacing step forward. "And I tend to get a little testy when I don't get my way. Remember Gloria Thorpe? Remember how I dealt with her when she decided to play in my playground, to try to seduce one of the guys I had a crush on?" She snickered and passed an unwavering and angry gaze over me. "I think she still wears a wig to this day." She reached out to finger the escaped blonde curl of hair. "And she had such lovely hair, didn't she?"

"Aren't you a little too old to be playing such high school games?"

"Nice attempt to put on a brave front, Laura, but I see it in your eyes... the fear, the questions, the uncertainty. But don't worry. I have no plans to cause you irreparable harm." She stepped closer and stood almost nose to nose with me. "I want to know what happened that night with Michael. I want to know every sordid little detail, but, more importantly, I want to know what Michael's last words were to you. I want to know what you two talked about on his last day on this earth. What did he say, Laura?"

"He didn't say anything..."

She shoved me back and grinned. "I can make you talk, Laura. You can either chose to have it easy, or have it hard, and I'll admit, I'd have no problem at all making it hard. I have half a mind to make it as painful as possible, just for spite… just a little payback for getting in the way to begin with."

"What are you…?" I couldn't even get the whole question out. I knew she had the capacity to be extremely cruel when crossed.

But I couldn't imagine what she had in mind.

# Chapter 8

Willow snapped her fingers and the door to the apartment opened.

"Jackson," I whispered in horror.

"Ah," Willow said with a wicked smile. "So you do remember Jackson Harris. I thought you might have forgotten all about him."

Clearly, she'd counted on my remembering him very well. And, how could I ever forget him? I'd spent the last few years trying to put him out of my mind, to move on with my life and forget the trembling young girl I'd been when I'd first met him, and the sexually wound up woman I'd become while under his possessive and obsessive control.

He looked just as good as he had back then; strong, sexy, vibrant and alluring. It'd been so easy to fall for him. Every girl wanted his attention and when he'd turned his attention to me, I gladly and willingly fell under his charm. But his charm soon turned to complete and utter control.

"Are your panties wet already, Laura?" Willow said with a snicker.

Now that she mentioned it, yes. I was instantly brought back to that summer; a summer of lush fields, intense heat and Southern charm in the countryside just east of Atlanta, Georgia. I'd accompanied my father that summer when he'd visited several farms in the area to find new suppliers... one of them had been Jackson's.

Jackson oozed charm and I'd been naïve enough to fall for it. But looking at him now, it was easy to see that he still had that charm. If anything it was even more intense, more magnetic. He still had that way of looking at a woman, looking deep into her soul, her body... deep in the cavity that harbored irrepressible lust and hunger, no matter how well brought up a young lady was. He was an animal underneath that southern gentleman polite veneer, and once he got you into his bed, you'd know he was going to ravage you. The thought of that had always made me hunger for him.

He'd been my first, and for the longest time, I'd wanted him to be my one and only... forever.

"It's good to see you again, sweet thing. It's been a long time."

Not long enough, I thought as a sting of want pierced through my panties and left a sharp ache between my thighs.

With just one hot and satisfying encounter, he'd turned me into a raging sex addict, unable to get enough, unable to concentrate or think of anything other than my next sexual encounter with him.

"Remember all those hot nights, baby? In the fields, in the barn, in the back of my truck, on my dining room table..." he smiled a slow and sexy smile that went straight to the core of me.

And those lazy, crazy days. There wasn't anything they hadn't tried.

"I've missed you. Sex isn't the same without you, girl."

I swallowed as he took a step closer. It'd taken so long to get over him. That summer had remained branded on my soul for the remainder of the year. I'd returned to California broken and itching to be with a man every minute of every day in order to forget how he made my body feel, how he made me crave him, how he made me think I couldn't go a day without him thrusting into me, without a man thrusting into me. I became insatiable because of him.

"It has been a long time," I managed to say without sounding too hungry.

"Five years. And you haven't changed a bit. So beautiful, so haughty. So full of restraint and control. I thought I'd broken you of that."

It certainly had been difficult regaining control. I decided to put on a brave face and not let him know just how hard it was to get over him. "I'm a lot stronger than I used to be. I've grown... matured."

"You were barely eighteen then. I would imagine you would indeed be strong now. Look at you. You're a pillar of strength."

He was mocking me. I could see it in his eyes, those deep, dark eyes that pulled me in and refused to let go. Why did he have such a hold on me? I'd met so many great men since breaking up with Jackson, including Michael, and yet he was the only one who had such an effect on me. Not even Michael had had such control over me.

Willow stepped aside as he came up to me, strong and determined to break me once again.

"Don't be so quick to mock me, Jackson. You may have caught me off guard, but I'm not the submissive girl you once knew. You brainwashed me once and made a puppet of me, but your Southern charm and boyish good looks won't work on me this time. I've moved on. I'm a little more worldly than the innocent little girl you took advantage of."

"From what I remember, you enjoyed the way I took advantage of you."

"The fact remains... I'm older and stronger."

"So I hear... a lawyer. Who would have thought?"

"If you'd listened to a word I said back then, you would have known. I've always wanted to be a lawyer. It's in my blood."

"No," he said as he leaned in closer. "Being my sex slave is in your blood. I'm sure you're already eager to take my cock into that sexy mouth of yours and suck me until I come all over you. Then you'd want me to bend you over and ram you hard from behind, not stopping until you've orgasm."

He'd always been good with dirty talk; just dirty enough to get me hot, to make me want him. I didn't even realized that Willow and Camille were no longer in the room, and I was alone with Jackson, looking me over like he could see every curve, every pore of my skin behind the sexy red dress I wore tonight. My legs tingled and standing upright became difficult, but I didn't want to give into him.

Surely I was better than that. Surely I'd learned a valuable lesson after that heartbreaking and difficult summer.

I would not allow myself to get caught up in his charm, in his game.

I would not become his slave again.

# Chapter 9

I knew I had to stop staring at Jackson, but my eyes were riveted to him. After all this time, I just couldn't believe he was there, in the flesh, and his eyes registered the same hunger for me that they had the last time I'd seen him.

My stomach turned over with fear and desire. He was the kind of guy who was so boyishly good looking yet virile. His broad shoulders, muscular arms and thick tree trunk legs filled out his black t-shirt and jeans tightly. He smelled like sex, like a man ready to hungry for sex. It was disarming how my body on a base feminine level responded with lust to him. After all this time…

"I've brought a few little gifts for our reunion." He walked to the kitchen table and pulled several items from a large leather duffle bag; heavy chains with iron cuffs, a long, narrow and very sharp looking knife and a flogger, complete with small metal spikes.

I couldn't imagine why he would bring such items. Yes, we had enjoyed playing such games a long, long time ago, but I'd left him and all the sordid games he came up with several years before. The items that might have aroused me while under his spell now looked like devices meant to torture.

"I remember how you liked it rough."

"That was a long time ago, Jackson. I've grown up since."

"This isn't exactly something you just grow out of, honey. This is who you are, what drives you on."

"Wrong. Maybe you stayed stuck in that world, but I've moved on."

He picked up the flogger and brushed it along the palm of his hand. "I don't think it would take much to draw you back into the world you belong to." Taking a few steps closer, he turned his palm up and flicked the spiked flogger into his hand.

I swallowed as his deepening tone reached inside me and touched something I'd long put away; something so carnal that I instinctively reacted to it. My body's reaction surprised me, it was so strong and determined.

But I was determined, too; to beat him this time and I would bite back whatever arousal he managed to pull out of me.

"You're still as sexy as I remember you, Laura… especially in that tight dress you're wearing."

Looking down at the beautiful dress I'd chosen, I frowned. I had dressed up to meet Peter Townshend, putting on my sex vixen vibe…not knowing it would be Jackson who would benefit from it.

"All you have to do is relax, angel." He reached out to run his fingers up my cheek and into my hair.

My mouth watered and my eyelids fell with sudden hunger. It had happened so many times before… falling under his spell, falling into a trance, a trance that left me unable to think logically while my body thrilled at his every touch, a trance in which all I wanted, all I craved was sex. It was enough to make me lose control. But when he slapped my thigh with the flogger, I remembered. I remembered how hard it'd been breaking away from him. I remembered all the times I'd lost control.

Damn it, but I wasn't ready to go back to that. Despite my body's eager and swift response, I gripped the flogger in my hand and stilled his motions. My eyes, hopefully as hardened as my heart, met his.

I can't waver, I thought. I have to stay strong and in control.

"Fuck off," I said in a tone that left no room for doubt. I did not want anything to do with him.

"I have… many times. Now I want to fuck you." He released the flogger from my grip and whipped it once again against my thigh.

It stung and burned, bringing with the pain a flood of memories I'd long ago set aside.

I was only eighteen when I became entangled in his wicked carnival of lusty games. How naïve I'd been. He made me believe having sex with him was love, that I was worthless unless I was desired by him, used in any which way to pleasure him. He twisted my naïve sheltered mind and heart into believing a woman's worth was what was between her legs and nothing else. He took away my self-esteem, stripped away whatever dignity I had when I was with him in his world, as his submissive.

As I stared at him, the horrors of those years as his sex slave came back to me. It stung to realize the actual acts still aroused me, still brought out something so feral and wanton in me. But I'd matured so much, mentally and emotionally. I no longer needed to have someone overpower me.

I had Chrissy to thank for that. At twenty-two, Chrissy had already been through a lot when she'd come to volunteer at the women's shelter. When I arrived two years later, a twenty year old wash out who was defeated and busted, she turned my life around.

She'd been through so much for someone so young. On countless nights after leaving the shelter, her voice would still ring in my ears, encouraging me and giving me strength.

"I went through more hell than you can imagine, Laura," she said not long after we met; her way of encouraging me to open up to her about my tormented relationship with Jackson. "And I had so much promise, everyone was sure I'd go on to be a super model or actress." She smiled a wistful smile that made me sad to see all she'd lost.

"When I was five, my mom entered me in one of those child beauty pageants," she went on. "I was thrilled. I loved the pretty dresses, the hair, the make-up. I loved the attention. And I was pretty good... you know, playing cute and hamming it up for the crowd. There were plenty of pageants that I lost and I'd cry the whole way home, but as I got older, I won more and more often. Soon my mom didn't know where to put all the trophies."

"That doesn't sound too hellish to me."

"It wasn't, until I got into my teens. By then my mom had become addicted to the whole process. She loved the adoration… and money was starting to look good, too. She pushed me into one pageant after another, and when she couldn't tag along, she put me in the hands of guardians… guardians who didn't give a shit what happened to me. Before I knew it, I was being offered alcohol and then drugs in every color of the rainbow. Like your typical teen, I thought it was cool. I thought I was cool. I mean, here I was with all these grown-ups and they were letting me into their circle."

"You got in with the wrong crowd?"

"The wrongest. And right smack in the middle of that wrongest crowd was the wrongest guy I could fall for."

"A good looking guy full of charm, I bet."

"You better believe it. He was the kind of guy who looked like a movie star. You know, the kind you'd plaster your walls with posters of. Man, he was cute, and I fell for him hook, line and sinker." When she looked at me, her eyes were full of understanding for what I'd been though. "I know what it's like to fall in love with a man who only wants to use you for his own pleasure. In my case, he also wanted to use me for the pleasure of others. In a moment of complete abandon, he convinced me to have our sexual exploits put on tape. He said he wanted to watch them when he missed me, when we were apart. I thought it was a cute idea, and of course, I was flattered."

"Oh, my God," I said, appalled by the idea.

"And, as you can imagine, this wasn't straight up, simple sex. I mean, we went wild, and, at the time, the wilder it got, the hornier I became. Knowing a camera was on us turned me on even more. I loved the idea... that is until he started selling our sexual encounters on the internet." She snorted a little sardonically and shot me a glance. "The money was pretty good. The very first month he sold for over three thousand dollars worth and within six months he was making a little over eleven thousand dollars a month. Not bad for an amateur, right?"

"I'll bet you didn't see much of that money."

She shrugged. "To keep me going, to encourage me to continue making tapes that were increasingly racy, he spoiled me those first few months. You know... a pretty dress here, a little lingerie there; a few nice dinners... good wine... all that shit, but it was really just peanuts compared to the money he was raking in. But, despite the money, all of it started to implode when people I knew got wind of the tapes. I was mortified. I mean, it's one thing to show my ass off in front of strangers, but when people you know start to look at you... you know. I tried to get out of it. I told him we'd made enough tapes, but he didn't want to hear about it. On tape, he raped me... and I don't mean just a rough and tough tumble in bed. He let me know he didn't like my decision."

I felt her pain as her eyes darkened with the memory.

"I ended up in the hospital with a fractured collar bone, a few stitches behind my ear and more bruises than I could count. But in the end, it turned out to be a good thing."

Taken aback, I stared at her. "Good thing? Are you a masochist or something?"

Her smile was suddenly serene and filled with wisdom. Twenty-four and she had her act together in a way that won my complete admiration. "It was what I needed to finally break away from him. And I never looked back. I initially came to this women's center to get my shit together, but it didn't take long for me to realize I was a lot stronger than most of the women in here."

I bit my lip as thoughts of Jackson invaded our conversation. Despite all I'd been through with him, despite the pain and humiliation, I still craved his touch. I felt stupid for wanting him, for wanting to please him. I could still taste his cock, still smell his skin, still feel his hands on my head as he pushed me repeatedly into his crotch.

"How long has it been since you've seen him?" Chrissy asked.

"A few months now."

"So you haven't had sex for a while. How do you feel?"

"It hasn't been as long as you think. I tried to forget all about Jackson by…"

"Sleeping with other men?"

Filled with shame, I nodded. "I tried to break out of the cycle, but I was continually drawn back in."

"Like a drug."

"Exactly. I finally thought I'd broken free of this drug when I met up with an old friend from high school; Michael. Even though we never hung out together in school - I was kind of shy around him - his father was a client of my father, and we happened to run into each other one night at a fund raiser." I smiled at the very thought of Michael. "You wouldn't believe how adorable he was. I mean, women literally fell at his feet and begged to bear his children, he was that good looking."

"So what happened? Did you guys hit it off?"

"Hit it off? We were inseparable - something that ticked his sister off to no end. Willow was just as possessive of her brother as she was of her beaus. In her little narcissistic mind, every man was meant only for her. But Michael didn't really pay attention to her requests - actually more like demands - that he stop seeing me."

"What was your relationship with him like?"

"Cool at first. I mean, I was completely blown over by him. I couldn't believe such a good looking guy could go for me... that and the fact that we weren't really from the same class of people. Don't get me wrong. My father did pretty well and we had a nice life, but it was nothing compared to the Brooks."

"Was that part of his charm? The money?"

I shrugged. "Not really. I mean, it was an added bonus, but all I was really interested in was the sex." Letting out a little laugh, I thought back to that night at the fund raiser. "I was so hungry for sex, so eager for gratification, I practically dragged him away from the crowd and into the club house. We found a dark and private corner and he didn't waste much time. He kissed me. You know. The kind of kiss you want to go on forever. But I wanted more than just a kiss. I wanted a fuck before we got caught. I was so damned scared of getting caught before he could satisfy the hunger in me."

"Sounds like you had it bad."

"Bad? But man was it good. With no time to waste, I had unzipped his pants and pulled out his large hard and eager cock. My God, it was beautiful. The skin so soft and smooth over the large shaft that was so hard, I'm sure it was painful for him. Immediately, I'd wanted to sooth that pain and release the tension."

I kissed the tip of his cock before putting it all in my mouth and sucking on it slow and steady. His knees buckled while his hands stayed steady in my hair, his fingers digging in whenever I pulled back and made him wait too long before taking him in again.

He shuddered with the need for release, but I kept him waiting until I thought he'd die from the explosion. His face had become a strange mask of tension as his oncoming orgasm drew all the blood down to the only part of his body that mattered at that very moment.

"Michael was a very good lover," I said to Chrissy. "But I was surprised to find how inexperienced he was. I mean, he knew all the regular, ho-hum moves, but he was very… safe."

"Are you the one who brought out the animal in him?"

I shook my head. "The animal was there. I think I just gave him the permission he needed to become that animal. He came from a pretty stiff family. They probably wouldn't have accepted his… preferences."

"So what turned the relationship sour?"

"In my fucked up head, I realized I could make him my sub; get him to do my bidding... anything I wanted."

"Sounds delightful."

"It was, until it became inadequate for him. He wanted more. The things he wanted me to do to him..." I closed my eyes as I remembered drawing blood with a whip I'd used on him. I'd immediately put a stop to the lashing, but he'd wanted more. "I mean, having him as my sub turned me on, but what he started asking for didn't turn me on at all. In fact, it repulsed me. I knew I had to put an end to it all. And I do mean all."

"That's how you ended up here?"

"It was bad enough I'd become a sex addict. I didn't want to be responsible for someone else falling into that trap."

"That's a pretty mature decision."

I looked at her, wondering if I truly had the maturity necessary to keep to that decision.

But, in the end, Chrissy was able to help me put all the various aspects of my life in order. I was able to compartmentalize certain wants and needs, and understand other desires. Soon, my desire to become a lawyer was what drove me.

A few years down the road and I was even able to help Serena when she admitted the hold Price still had on her.

And now, my career as a lawyer was just about to take off. The road to litigation hadn't been easy, and Jackson had put up a few hurdles here and there. He'd stalked me, called me, pursued me until I was sure I'd succumb to him, but I never did.

But he was putting up another hurdle, his very presence was enough to leave me frozen in place. Fear, doubt, want and a tireless sex drive all swirled through me, confusing me.

Jackson approached me and ran his hand down my thighs, sending a shiver of both fear and excitement through me. "I've grown my collection of toys since we've last fucked, and I can't wait to use them all on you, maybe even all at once while I lick your tits and jam a few of these…" he glanced over at an assortment of long and colorful objects in his bag.

I gulped. Years ago, I would have salivated over his words alone describing what he'd do to me, but now, he seemed more extreme than ever, and I didn't know how to fight him off.

Worse, I had to fight to keep control of myself or everything I fought hard for would be in vain. And, I would not only be implicated for the murder of Michael Brooks, but Serena may lose everything, too, including Sebastian.

### This is the End of Part I

### Thank you for reading BARELY LEGAL Vol. 1.

### Part 2 is now available where books are sold.

### *Barely Legal*

\*\*\*\*\*

*The Barely Legal Series* features some characters from *The Protégé Trilogy*

**For 18 and Up**

**A quick read, all three books in The Protégé Trilogy is complete and available everywhere.**

If you liked *Barely Legal*, you would like

## The Blue Room Series

When Danny Blue of the Never Knights inherited his playboy billionaire father's businesses and legacy, he didn't realized his father's pet project was the Blue Room, the most elite and secret club in the highest circle. He was happy to let his half-brother Terrence Blue run the club, but with Terrence's womanizing ways and carefree attitude when it came to everything, he wasn't sure if that was a good idea.

Terrence Blue wasn't sure that was a good idea as well because it would cramp his style as a former patron of the club, but when he spotted virginal Staci Atussi starting at The Blue Room, he had a change of heart. Not only was Staci Atussi a knockout without knowing it, but she was the challenge he had been craving.

For Staci Atussi, working at The Blue Room was her solution to a desperate situation, but as she became integrated into the world of The Blue Room and the mysteries surrounding its patrons and the sexy Blues, she wondered if she had traded in her desperation for something far more sinister.

The Blue Room is a New Adult Contemporary Suspense Series intended for readers age 18 and up.

# Other Adult Romance Series from Sparklesoup Authors

## Master Chefs Series

## HEAT Serial

## Kings of Fire Series

## Loving Summer Series

## Hidden Falls High Series

## Inner Circle Series

## Never Knights Trilogy

Barely Legal (Barely Legal Vol. #1)

## Blue Room Serial

## Blue Room Confidentials

## Saints of San Angelo U.

## The Protégé

## Barely Legal Serial

## Sessions Serial

## Filthy Dirty Laundry

## You & Me Trilogy

## Rock Hard Musical

## Drama Diaries Standalone Novels

## Beautiful Girl: A Beauty and Beast Re-telling

## Shadowlight Academy

## Shadowlight Hunters Academy

## Vampire Samurai Series

## Society of Supernatural Sleuths

## M.A.G.E. Series

## Magical World Series

## Fallen Fae Academy

## Fae B. I. Series

## Cruel Princes of Wyvern Academy

## Ruthless Reign Series

## Bad Boys Billionaire Bachelors Club

## The More the Merrier RH Series

## Baby Girl Series

## Bad Boys Royals of Kingsbury Prep

## Kingmakers of Kingsbury

## Prickly Proposal

Kailin Gow

# HOUSE Series

# Heartbreak Falls Series

# The Bully Who Loved Me

## OTHER ROMANTIC COMEDIES
## BOOKS

**BOSSY BODYGUARD by Sunny Winters**

**COCKY COP by Sunny Winters**

**AFTERNOON DELIGHT by D.R. LOVE**

Barely Legal (Barely Legal Vol. #1)


TONGUE TIED by D.R. LOVE


JUNK by D.R. LOVE


EATING VELVET by D.R. LOVE


STEPBROTHER FIGHTER by Rachel Angel


OH MY! RAPTURE by A.B. Binds

# Sign Up for My Adult Romance Newsletter

No spam. No ham. We only send you up-to-date information about new releases, new series, series updates, contests, author events and more at:

Steamy Adult Books